Periwinkle Smith

and the Faraway Star

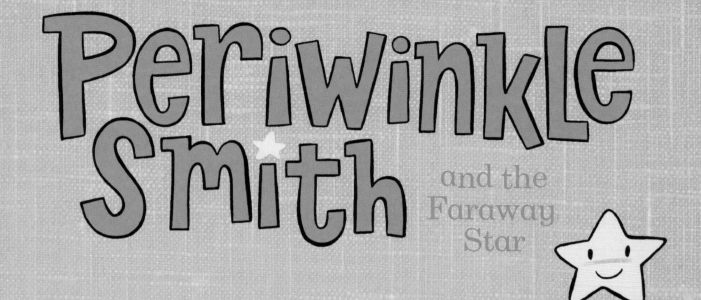

by John&wendy

PSS!
PRICE STERN SLOAN

An Imprint of Penguin Group (USA) Inc.

Periwinkle Smith loved looking
through her shiny gold telescope.

She looked at birds.

She looked at fish.

She looked at enemy pirates.

Every night before bed, she looked at the stars. She loved how they twinkled and winked at one another. It was like they were playing a game in the sky.

One night she spotted a star who
wasn't playing with the others.
He was all by himself and she
thought he looked very lonely.

Periwinkle thought and thought. Maybe if *she* were the star's friend, he wouldn't be lonely anymore. She decided to make friends with the faraway star.

So Periwinkle wrote him a letter.

And she found the perfect way to send it.

UP

But her letter didn't reach
the faraway star.

So Periwinkle painted him a picture.

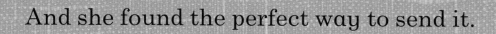

And she found the perfect way to send it.

UP

But her picture
didn't reach the
faraway star.

So Periwinkle decided to deliver the message herself.

And she built the perfect way to do it.

UP

But Periwinkle Smith couldn't reach the faraway star.

Periwinkle worried that she would *never* make friends with the star.

Just then
she saw a light.

Suddenly Periwinkle knew just how to get her message to the faraway star! She grabbed her paint and her flashlight and got to work.

Red

Then she went to the window
and turned on her flashlight.

UP

UP

UP

And her message finally reached
the faraway star.

For Brooke and Bonnie,
and all stargazers big and small.

PRICE STERN SLOAN
Published by the Penguin Group
Penguin Group (USA) Inc., 375 Hudson Street, New York, New York 10014, USA
Penguin Group (Canada), 90 Eglinton Avenue East, Suite 700,
Toronto, Ontario M4P 2Y3, Canada
(a division of Pearson Penguin Canada Inc.)
Penguin Books Ltd., 80 Strand, London WC2R 0RL, England
Penguin Group Ireland, 25 St. Stephen's Green, Dublin 2, Ireland
(a division of Penguin Books Ltd.)
Penguin Group (Australia), 250 Camberwell Road, Camberwell,
Victoria 3124, Australia
(a division of Pearson Australia Group Pty. Ltd.)
Penguin Books India Pvt. Ltd., 11 Community Centre,
Panchsheel Park, New Delhi—110 017, India
Penguin Group (NZ), 67 Apollo Drive, Rosedale, North Shore 0632, New Zealand
(a division of Pearson New Zealand Ltd.)
Penguin Books (South Africa) (Pty.) Ltd., 24 Sturdee Avenue,
Rosebank, Johannesburg 2196, South Africa

Penguin Books Ltd., Registered Offices: 80 Strand, London WC2R 0RL, England

Library of Congress Cataloging-in-Publication data is available.

ISBN 978-0-8431-9940-6   10 9 8 7 6 5 4 3 2 1